YOUTH EVERLASTING

AND OTHER ROMANIAN FAIRY TALES

PETRE ISPIRESCU

Translated by

ALEXA J ISPAS

CONTENTS

INTRODUCTION

WRITTEN BY ALEXA J ISPAS (TRANSLATOR)

The book you are about to read contains four tales that were originally collected and published in Romania during the second half of the 19th century by Petre Ispirescu.

I have translated these tales into English and adapted them for a contemporary audience.

Youth Everlasting, the first tale, is the most well-known and thought-provoking of all the fairy tales collected and published by Petre Ispirescu.

This tale starts with an intriguing premise: a baby refusing to come into the world until he is promised youth everlasting and life without death by his father.

When he grows older and his father cannot

keep his promise, the boy decides to take matters into his own hands and attempt to change his mortal destiny.

In the second tale, *The Rabbit, the Fox, the Wolf, and the Bear*, two young children are sent to the woods by their evil stepmother to die.

But as all hope seems lost, the creatures of the forest and their own resourcefulness help them find their way out.

Although this tale seems to start in similar way to *Hansel and Gretel*, this story follows a different trajectory, with many twists and turns along the way.

In the third tale, *The Magic Tree*, a young shepherd uses his cunning to reach the top of an enormous tree that nobody else has been able to climb.

But even though he initially appears to succeed in his mission, he soon discovers that finding his way back requires him to acquire a whole new set of skills.

In the fourth of the tales, *The Golden Children*, two young children are killed at birth while their mother is unjustly punished.

This tragic beginning sets the stage for a beautiful tale of rebirth and renewal, as the children re-appear and make their presence known in a variety of ways until justice is done.

If this is the first book you are reading in this series, please allow me a few moments to tell you a little bit about the background to these four stories.

They are part of a larger collection of stories that were first published in 19th century Romania, though they may have originated at an even earlier time.

Petre Ispirescu, the collector of these tales, was born in 1830, had grown up among Romanian fairy tales, and had taken up a job at a publishing house.

His first published collection dates from 1862, and he continued publishing Romanian fairy tales until close to his death, two decades later.

A couple of the stories he collected and published are part of the literature curriculum in Romanian schools, which is how I first came across them.

Yet many of them are unknown to most Romanian people.

They had certainly been unknown to me, until I accidentally stumbled upon *Ileana*

Samziana a while ago, many years after having moved from my native Romania to start a new life in the UK.

I retitled that story *The Girl Who Would Be King* and you can find it as the first story in a book by the same name that is part of this series.

I was so surprised and amazed by that story (a transgender fairy tale dating from at least the 19th century Romania!) that I made my way through Petre Ispirescu's entire collection.

I loved the stories in that collection so much that I decided to translate and adapt them for an English-speaking, contemporary audience, and publish them as a series of short, easy-to-read books.

In doing so, I did my best to stay true to the narrative heart of each story, yet filter out elements of racial discrimination and other such aspects that do not sit well with my 21st century values.

I have also taken creative license with many of the titles, as well as with the sentence structure and length.

Following each tale, I have included a *Translator's Note* in which I summarize the changes I have made, for any readers who would like to know more about how my translated and adapted version differs from the original.

I have also used that section to add short pieces of personal commentary focused on various aspects of the story, as well as to point readers to related tales or other relevant resources that may be of interest.

This type of direct message from the translator to the reader is rather unusual in translated works, but I hope that readers will enjoy the transparency and added insight these sections provide.

As such, the books in the *Romanian Stories* series also represent an experiment in the art of putting together a translated version of a piece of work.

If you enjoy these stories, you can find more at www.storybothy.com

YOUTH EVERLASTING

Once upon a time, there was a king and queen who had trouble conceiving a child.

They went to healers and astrologers to find a way to have a child, but it was all in vain.

Eventually, the king heard of a knowing old man in a village close-by and he sent messengers to invite the old man to the palace.

But the old man sent the messengers back, saying that whoever needs his services should come to him.

So the king and queen took a few of their servants, soldiers, and counsellors with them and went to the old man's house.

The old man, seeing them from afar, came out to greet them.

"Welcome, your Majesty," the old man said, "what are you wanting to find? The wish you have will bring you sadness."

"I came to ask if you can give us something that will help us have children."

"I can," the old man said, "you will have one son, but you will not be able to enjoy him for long."

The king and queen dismissed the old man's warning.

They took the medicine he had given them and returned to the palace.

Several days later, the queen found herself pregnant.

The entire kingdom and everyone at court rejoiced at the news.

During the queen's labor, the child started to cry so loudly, no healer could pacify him.

The king started promising him all the riches he possessed, but this did not work either.

"Keep quiet, daddy's little boy," the king was saying, "and I'll give you that kingdom and that kingdom. Keep quiet, and I'll give you that king's daughter or that other king's daughter as a wife," and many such promises.

In the end, seeing that he will not keep quiet, the king said:

"Keep quiet, my son, and I will give you youth everlasting and life without death."

Then, the child went quiet and got born.

The servants sounded the trumpets and the celebrations lasted an entire week.

The older the boy grew, the cleverer and more daring he became.

His parents sent him to schools and philosophers, and all the teachings that children usually learn within a year, he would learn within a month.

The king was bursting with pride, and the inhabitants of the kingdom were delighted to have an heir to the throne as wise and gifted as Solomon the King.

For a while however, even though still looking healthy, the boy seemed sad and deep in thought.

On his fifteenth birthday, the king was having a celebratory meal with his counsellors and the servants of the kingdom.

As they were having fun, the boy, who was now known as Prince Charming, got up and said:

"Dad, the time has come for you to give me what you promised at birth."

Great sadness overcame the king upon hearing this.

"My son," the king said, "how can I give you something that does not exist? I only made you that promise to appease you."

"Then I will travel the world until I fulfill the promise under which I was born."

All the aristocrats and the king pleaded with him, asking him to stay.

"Your father is getting older," the aristocrats were saying, "and we want to instate you as king in his stead. We will bring the most beautiful queen under the sun as your wife."

But there was no way to overturn Prince Charming's decision.

He remained solid as a rock in his determination.

Realizing that there was no way to change his son's mind, the king gave his permission.

He asked that preparations be made for his son's travels.

Prince Charming went to the royal stables, where the most beautiful steeds were kept, to choose one for himself.

But none of the horses could withstand his strength.

He would grab each one by the tail and toss them to the side as if they were rag dolls.

In the end, when he was about to leave, he took one last look through the stables.

Suddenly he spotted, in one of the corners, a horse that was thin and full of scabs.

Prince Charming decided to test this horse as well.

When he grabbed the horse's tail, the horse turned around and said:

"What do you command, master? Thank God that I have lived long enough to have a hero put his hands on me again."

And strengthening his legs, the horse stood straight as a candle.

Prince Charming told him what he had in mind.

"To fulfill your wish," the horse said, "you have to ask your dad for his shield, his spear, his bow, his quiver, and his clothes from when he was a young man. And you have to boil my oats in milk and restore me to health with your own fair hand over the course of six weeks."

Prince Charming asked the king for all the things the horse had suggested.

The king called the treasury keeper and asked him to open all the court's trunks, where the royal clothes and weapons were kept, so his son could choose the ones he wanted.

Prince Charming searched through the trunks for three days and three nights.

At last he found, at the bottom of an old trunk, the weapons and clothes that had belonged to his father when he had been a young lad.

The weapons were all rusty, so he started cleaning them up himself.

Within six weeks, he succeeded in making the weapons shine so brightly, he could see his reflection in them as in a mirror.

During this time, he also took care of the horse the way the horse had told him to do.

All this was hard and tedious work, but in the end, it was done.

Prince Charming told the horse that the clothes and the weapons are clean and ready.

The horse shook himself and all the boils and scabs fell off him.

Not only did he look like a young, beautiful horse, but he also had four wings.

"We will leave in three days time," Prince Charming said.

On the morning of the third day, the members of the royal court and all the inhabitants of the kingdom were full of sorrow.

Prince Charming was dressed like a warrior, holding his sword in his hand and riding the horse he had chosen.

He said his goodbyes to the king and queen, to the courtiers, to the soldiers, and to all the court servants.

Everyone had tears in their eyes and kept asking him not to undertake the trip, so as not to endanger himself.

But he spurred on his horse and went out of the gate as fast as the wind.

After him came a long line of carriages with food, money, and about two hundred soldiers, whom the king had selected to accompany him.

After he crossed the borders of his father's kingdom and reached empty land, Prince Charming stopped for a break.

He divided all his belongings among the

soldiers and kept for himself only as much food as his horse could carry.

Then, taking his goodbyes, he sent his soldiers back to his father's kingdom.

He took the road leading to the East, and rode for three days and three nights.

Eventually he reached a valley where he came across a pile of human bones.

While taking a rest, his horse told him:

"We have arrived on the lands of the Witch. She is so evil that she kills anyone who dares to tread on her property. She was once a woman like all women, but she was cursed by her parents to turn into a witch. At this moment she is with her children. But tomorrow, in the forest which you can see, we will meet her because she will come to kill you. She is extremely large and menacing. But don't be afraid, be ready with your bow to shoot arrows at her. Hold your sword and your spear close at hand, to use them at the right moment."

They went to sleep, taking turns to keep watch.

The next day, at dawn, they got ready to ride through the forest.

Prince Charming tightened the horse's harness more than before, and they set off.

Suddenly, they heard a terrible rumbling.

"Hold on tight, master," the horse said, "the Witch is approaching."

She was moving so fast that trees were falling in her wake as she came towards them.

But Prince Charming and the horse were prepared for her attack.

The horse went up like the wind, hovering over her, and Prince Charming pierced one of her legs with an arrow.

When he was about to aim a second arrow at her, she shouted:

"Wait, Prince Charming, I surrender!"

Seeing he does not believe her, she acknowledged his victory in writing with her own blood.

"May your horse live long years from now, Prince Charming," she said. "If it hadn't been for him, I would have swallowed you whole. Now it is you who has defeated me. Up until this day, no mortal has come this far. A few crazy fools who dared to try have only made it as far as the valley where you saw the pile of bones."

She invited them to her home, where she

gave Prince Charming food and treated him like an honored guest.

While they were eating, the Witch was moaning from pain.

He took out her leg, which he had kept in his bag, and put it back in its place, where it immediately healed.

The Witch was so happy she cooked a feast that lasted three whole days.

She also introduced him to her three daughters, who were as beautiful as fairies, and offered him to take one of them as his wife.

Prince Charming declined, and told her about his quest.

"With the horse that you have and your bravery," she said, "I think you will succeed."

After three days, they got ready to continue their journey.

After they left the lands of the Witch, they reached a beautiful valley.

The grass on one side was green and vibrant, while on the other side it was burnt.

"Why is the grass burnt?" Prince Charming asked his horse.

"We have arrived on the lands of the Scorpy," the horse answered, "the Witch's sister. The two of them are so evil, they cannot live in the same place. The curse of their parents has reached them, and that's why they have transformed into beasts, as you have seen. Their rivalry is terrible, they are constantly trying to steal land from one another. When the Scorpy is angry, she spills fire and tar. It seems she has recently had a fight with her sister and, wanting to chase her off her land, has burnt the grass where her sister had stood. She is even more evil than her sister and has three heads. Let us rest a little, as we will have to face her early in the morning."

The next day they got themselves ready, as they had when they had met the Witch, and set off.

Suddenly, they started hearing a scream and a rumbling as they had never heard before.

"Get ready, master, the Scorpy is coming."

The Scorpy was spilling flames and approaching as fast as the wind, with one jaw in the sky and one touching the ground.

The horse swiftly rose in the air and hovered above her.

Prince Charming took off one of her heads with an arrow.

He was about to aim another arrow at her, to

take off another head, when the Scorpy surrendered.

She asked him to forgive her and promised she won't do him any harm.

To gain his trust, she wrote the promise in her own blood.

The Scorpy laid a feast for Prince Charming even more plentiful than the Witch had done.

And he returned her head, which stuck itself back into place.

After three days, they went on their way.

Reaching the end of the Scorpy's lands, they went, and went, and went some more.

Eventually they reached a field full of the most enchanting flowers.

A slight breeze was flowing through, and they decided to stop for a rest.

"We have managed to get this far, master," the horse said. "Yet we still have one big hurdle to overcome. We will go through great peril. And if God will help us to get through that, we will achieve our aim. We are close to the palace where Youth Everlasting lives. The palace is surrounded by a forest thick and tall, inhabited by the wildest animals that live on this earth. Day and night they stand guard, and there are many of them. There is no way to fight them. We will have to try to fly over them."

After resting for two days, they got ready for the next stage of their journey.

"Master, tighten the harness as much as you can," the horse said, "and when you straddle me, hold yourself tight, grabbing my mane. Hold your feet glued to my body, so you do not get dizzy."

Prince Charming did as his horse had told him to do.

They started flying through the air, and soon they were close to the forest.

"Master," the horse said, "at this very moment, food is being given to the beasts of the forest and they are gathered in the yard. Let us pass."

They rose into the air and saw the palace, which shone brighter than the sun.

Just as they were about to land, Prince Charming brushed his foot against the top of a tree.

The entire forest immediately started swaying, and the beasts began screaming so loudly, it would make you lose your hearing.

If the lady of the palace had not been outside, feeding her babies, which is what she called the beasts of the forest, they would have devoured our two travelers.

She rescued them, because she had never seen another human being around her place, and she was delighted they had come.

When Prince Charming saw her extraordinary beauty, he was glued to the spot.

"Welcome, Prince Charming!" she said. "What are you looking for around here?"

"I am looking," he said, "for Youth Everlasting," he said

"In that case, you have found her."

Prince Charming got off his horse and entered the palace.

There he found two other women, Youth Everlasting's older sisters.

He thanked the fairy for saving him from danger and she cooked him a tasty meal and put it in golden bowls.

The three sisters let the horse eat grass from wherever he may wish, and introduced Prince Charming to the wild beasts, so he could go through the forest in peace.

The women asked him to move in with them, as they had grown tired living by themselves.

He gladly accepted their invite, as one who had been seeking this.

Day by day, they started getting used to one another.

He told them his story and all the things he had been through to reach them.

Soon after, he wed the youngest of the three women.

At their wedding, the ladies of the house gave him permission to go wherever he wished.

Only through a valley, which they called the Valley of Sorrows, they told him not to go.

They warned him that things would not go well for him if he did.

Time passed, even though he was oblivious to it.

Age had forgotten about him, so he stayed just as young as the day of his arrival.

He was passing through the forest unharmed, enjoying the golden palaces, and living in peace and tranquility with his wife and sisters-in-laws.

He was delighting in the beauty of the flowers and the sweetness and cleanliness of the air.

To entertain himself, he would go hunting.

One day, he started chasing a rabbit.

He aimed an arrow at the rabbit, but missed.

A second arrow caught the rabbit, but in the thrill of the chase, he inadvertently set foot into the Valley of Sorrows.

After he returned home, he became overwhelmed by homesickness and longed to see his mum and dad.

He did not dare to tell the fairies, but they realized it, seeing the grief and restlessness that had descended upon him.

"You have set foot into the Valley of Sorrows," they said to him with sadness in their eyes.

"I did, my dears, without meaning to do it. And now I am longing for my parents, yet I do not want to leave you. Even though I have only been here a few days, I love everything about this place. I will go see my parents one last time, and then I will come back here and never leave."

"Do not go," they said. "Your parents have died hundreds of years ago. If you leave, you will die as well."

But neither the women's pleas nor his horse's soothing words could make his homesickness go away.

"I have a suggestion," the horse said. "I can

take you back, as long as you agree to return straight away. But if you wish to stay for even one hour, I will return here without you."

Prince Charming agreed and they got ready to leave.

They hugged the women, said their good-byes, and set off, leaving them sighing and with tears in their eyes.

They reached the place where the lands of the Scorpy had been, but there they found cities.

The forest had been transformed into fields.

They asked here and there about the Scorpy and where they might find her.

But everyone they asked told them they had only heard about her from their elders, who would tell them made-up stories about the exis-tence of such a creature.

"How is that possible?" Prince Charming said. "We only passed through here the other day."

He tried telling them all he knew about the Scorpy, but the locals were laughing at him, as you would laugh at someone who is fantasizing or dreaming with open eyes.

Frustrated, he continued his journey, barely

noticing that his beard and his hair had turned white.

When they reached the lands of the Witch, he asked around as he did on the Scorpy's lands, and received similar answers.

He could not understand.

How had so many things changed in just a few days?

And once again, frustrated, he left, his white beard coming down to his chest and his legs shaking.

Eventually, they reached his father's lands.

Here he found different people, different cities, and the old ones had changed so much he no longer recognized them.

In the end, they arrived at the palace where he had been born.

As soon as he dismounted, the horse said:

"Master, I will now return to the place we have left. If you wish to return as well, jump back on and let's go!"

"Go in peace, I will join you as soon as I can."

The horse left as quick as lightning.

The palaces had been demolished and there were weeds protruding through the walls.

He was looking around with tears in his eyes,

trying to remember how brightly they once shone and how he had spent his childhood running through them.

He went round two or three times, looking through every room, every nook and cranny that reminded him of those things that had passed.

He then went down into the cellar, where the entrance had been covered by the debris from the demolition.

Searching here and there, his white beard coming down to his knees, lifting his eyelids with his hands and barely able to walk, he found an old, decrepit trunk.

He opened it, but did not find anything inside.

"Welcome," a tired voice said. "If you had taken any longer, even I would have died."

Death slapped his face, which had dried up like a prune.

He fell into the trunk, and immediately turned to dust.

And I jumped into a saddle and told you the story thus.

This tale's original title is 'Tinerete fara batranete si viata fara de moarte', which translates as 'Youth without old age and life without death'.

In Romania, this is the most well-known of all the stories collected and published by Petre Ispirescu.

I remember studying this tale in school in great detail, as it was part of the Romanian literature curriculum.

I suspect that Petre Ispirescu spent more time than usual polishing this tale to bring out its full potential, as it does not have the raw (and sometimes rushed) quality of many of his other tales.

The theme of immortality, which is what this

story is about, holds an important place in Romanian literature, and is often found in Romanian folklore.

You can find it, for example, in the *Miorita*, a folk poem about a young shepherd who is warned that his companions are plotting to murder him.

Instead of planning how to defend himself, the young shepherd considers all the ways he will live on by becoming part of the natural environment after his death.

You will also find this theme in the Romanian legend *Mesterul Manole*, in which a master stonemason attempts to build a church more beautiful than any other, as a legacy to his genius and his patron's generosity in funding the project.

Yet when the building repeatedly crumbles due to a curse, Manole chooses to trap his pregnant wife into the walls of the church in order to secure his legacy and therefore ensure his immortality.

If you are interested in another story collected by Petre Ispirescu that focuses on the theme of immortality, I recommend reading *Death's Call*, also one of the Petre Ispirescu's tales, about a man who uses his enormous wealth to relocate to a country where there is no death.

If that premise sounds intriguing, you can find *Death's Call* in *The Girl Who Would Be King and Other Romanian Fairy Tales*.

As you have been reading *Youth Everlasting*, you may have wondered about the use of the title 'Prince Charming'.

The original version of this title is 'Fat Frumos', which is a name often given to the male hero in Romanian fairy tales.

A literal translation might be 'Handsome Youth' or 'Lad Handsome' (*frumos* means 'handsome' and *fat* refers to a young man).

I chose to translate this title as 'Prince Charming' as this is a well-known way to refer to a male hero in the English language.

THE RABBIT, THE FOX, THE WOLF, AND THE BEAR

There was once a man who had two children, a little boy and a little girl.

The children's mother had died, and the devil had goaded him to marry a second time.

His new wife couldn't stand the children.

There wasn't morning, or evening, or moment given by God when she wouldn't embitter their lives.

She would nag them, beat them up, or chase them away.

The children didn't know what to do to please her, but in vain.

One day, the woman told her husband:

"Unless you take your children somewhere in the wilderness, to let them die, I will leave you."

"How can I kill my own children?" the husband said.

"I don't care how you do it. Do what I say, or else."

What could the poor man do?

If he didn't do as she said, she would make his life a misery, and he was already losing the will to live.

But he felt pity for his children.

Eventually, he decided to do as she said, because her nagging would make him lose his wits.

He got up one morning and told his children they were going to gather some wood in the forest.

The girl, being the elder of the two, took two fistfuls of cornmeal in her apron and scattered it on the way.

When they got to the forest, their father made a fire, and said:

"Look children, I made you a fire. Stay here and get warm while I go cut some wood. I will bring you apples when I return."

"All right, dad," the children replied, "but come back soon. We are scared on our own."

The man left.

A short distance away he climbed into a tree and tied the end of a piece of wood from the top of the tree.

Whenever the wind would blow, the piece of wood would bang against the tree.

"Listen, that's dad cutting wood," the girl would say to the boy, to reassure him.

The man returned to his wife and told her what he had done.

When evening came, the man and his wife lay the table and ate.

As they had some crumbs left, the wife said:

"If the children were here, they could have eaten what we've got left."

"Here we are, here we are," the children said.

And they came out from their hiding place and ate.

After the children's father left the table, the stepmother asked them how they had managed to find their way back.

The girl told her how they had followed the trace of cornmeal she had scattered on their way into the forest.

Then they had hidden behind the fireplace once they got home, fearing she would be angry and beat them up.

Some time passed, and the stepmother kept nagging her husband to kill his children.

And being driven out of his wits, the children's father took his children to the forest once again.

The girl wanted to take some cornmeal again but didn't find any.

She went to the fireplace to take some ashes, but the stepmother hit her hand with a poker.

As they got into the forest, their father made a fire and left them there to go cut some wood.

The children waited, but he did not return.

When they saw that their father is not coming back, they went towards where he had gone, to look for him.

And when they couldn't find him, they stumbled their way through the forest until evening.

The boy, being younger, started wailing from tiredness and hunger.

The girl started wailing as well, because she didn't know what to give him to eat and where they could find some rest.

They kept walking and searching, and then returning to the fire their father had left them.

The sun had set without them having eaten or slept.

So the girl, to settle her brother down and get him to sleep, threw a cowpat, which she had found lying about, into the fire.

"Be quiet, little brother," she said. "Look, I have put some bread into the fire to bake. In the meantime, put your head in my lap and have a little rest."

The boy believed his sister and fell asleep.

After a while, an old man appeared.

"Hello, young ones," he said. "What do you have there in the fire?" the old man asked.

"Nothing," the girl said. "I have thrown a cowpat into the fire and have told my brother I am baking bread, to get him to sleep. He is shattered from hunger and tiredness."

After he sat there a while, the old man said to take the bread out of the fire, because it might be ready.

The girl was too tired to argue and took it out.

She couldn't believe her eyes when she found real bread in the fire.

When the girl saw this miracle, she got scared.

She knew what she had thrown into the fire, and she could see what she had taken out.

They all started to eat.

Even though they kept eating, there was always more bread to be eaten.

Then the old man took a strand of hair from the girl's hair.

He made a little bow out of the hair, gave it to the boy, and said:

"With this you can catch birds, so you have something to eat with the bread."

"Thank you, old man, thank you," both answered in one voice.

The old man taught the boy how to use the net and the bow, and then he left.

The boy started going through the forest catching birds.

He would bring the birds to his sister to cook, and in this way they were able to eat as much as they needed.

As they grew older, they got tired of putting their hands through tree holes and bushes.

They would have liked to find a place to rest their head.

While hunting one day, the boy came upon a rabbit.

He pulled out his bow to strike an arrow.

"Don't kill me, young man," the rabbit said.

"If you let me live, I will give you one of my young to serve you."

The boy did as the rabbit asked and took one of his young.

A little later he came upon a fox.

The fox said the same as the rabbit, and he took one of her young.

He later came upon a wolf, and the same thing happened, so he took one of the wolf's young.

He did the same when he came upon a bear.

Now the boy had four wild animal cubs, which he called his puppies.

He returned to his sister with his puppies in tow and took great care of them.

One day, the sister had an idea.

"Climb a tall tree," she told her brother, "and look in all directions, in case you see anything resembling a village."

She was tired of walking through the forest every day, forsaken by God.

The boy climbed the tallest tree he could find.

"I can't see anything," he said. "But in this direction further ahead, something is glowing white. I don't know what it is because it is too far away."

"Let's go and find out," the girl said.

After they walked for a day, he climbed another tall tree.

He looked in the same direction and thought he could see some houses.

They walked as fast as they could until they reached the place.

When they got there, what did they see?

Some palaces fit for a king, which belonged to a *zmeu*, a fearsome human-like creature with magic powers.

They went in but didn't see anyone.

The girl started dusting, cleaning, and putting everything in its place.

She also cooked some food, which they ate, and then they hid in one of the rooms.

In the evening, the *zmeu* returned home.

He saw that things were cleaner and tidier than he had left them.

"Whoever has done this for me, I would like to repay their kindness," he said.

They came out from hiding, and the girl said:

"I have wiped and cleaned."

The *zmeu* was delighted.

They set the table, ate together, and went to sleep.

The next day, the boy took his dogs and went hunting, because that was his task.

The *zmeu* did the same.

In the evening when they returned, they found the food ready.

They ate together and rejoiced.

After a while, the *zmeu* started returning from the hunt before the boy.

He had mellowed while spending time in the girl's company.

Day after day, the *zmeu* started to feel that his heart was pounding when he was around the girl, or when she smiled and spoke to him.

He gradually lost his passion for hunting and was looking for all sorts of reasons to stay home and spend time with the girl.

In turn, the girl started enjoying the *zmeu*'s company more and more each day.

The boy was minding his own business and didn't notice that things were changing at home.

As time passed, the *zmeu* and the girl started resenting the boy's presence.

They felt that he was a barrier to their blossoming romance.

But he did neither see nor hear what was going on between the *zmeu* and his sister.

He was unaware of their whispers and did not realize they had started playing tricks on him.

He would believe them when they said that he had come home too late and they had already eaten, so the food wouldn't spoil.

He would simply eat whatever he could find without complaint.

Or his sister would get angry at his puppies when the *zmeu* would try to woo her and the puppies would get in the way.

One day, the *zmeu* and the boy's sister decided that the only way to be free to pursue their romance was to kill the boy.

The *zmeu* wanted to go into the forest after him and eat him.

"Don't go," she told him, "because his puppies will tear you to pieces."

"Then how should we proceed?"

"Leave it to me to arrange things. I will tell you what to do."

She started to complain to her brother that she is feeling lonely at home on her own and asked him to leave her his puppies to keep her company.

Initially her brother didn't agree, because he had gotten used to having his puppies with him at all times.

But after much pleading, he took pity on his sister and left home without his puppies.

His sister took the four animals, shoved them into a mountain cave, and asked the *zmeu* to place a boulder at the exit.

Then the *zmeu* went into the forest to look for the boy.

When he saw the *zmeu* from afar coming towards him, the boy climbed up a tree.

"Come down so I can eat you," said the *zmeu*.

"You may eat me. But first, let me sing a song from when I was young," the boy answered.

"Go on then, but sing quickly, because I have no time to lose."

The boy sang:

"Can't hear,

can't see,

the heaviness of the earth,

and the lightness of the wind,

my puppies,

because your master is dying."

"Now get down so I can eat you," said the *zmeu*.

"Wait a little longer," the boy replied, "I want to sing another song."

He gave the *zmeu* a shoe to gnaw on, to appease him.

The boy sang the same song again.

Then he gave the *zmeu* his other shoe, and sang the song a third time.

As nothing was happening, he gave him his hat to gnaw on so he could sing a fourth time.

When he sang the first time, the rabbit heard him.

"Listen, brothers," he said, "our master is dying."

"Shut up, dishcloth ears," the fox said to him and slapped his face. "Don't tell lies about our master."

When the boy sang a second time, the fox heard.

She said the same as the rabbit, but the wolf slapped her across the face and told her as she had told the rabbit.

When the boy sang a third time, the wolf heard.

And as he said the same as the fox, the bear

slapped him across the face for lying that something bad had happened to their master.

But when he sang the fourth time, the bear heard as well.

The rabbit started to whimper that he had been unjustly treated.

"Leave the justice till later," the bear said. "Now let's get to work. Let's all join forces. We need to shift this rock so we can rescue our master."

The rabbit tried, but it made no difference.

The fox added her strength, and it seemed like something may be happening.

The wolf added his strength, and the rock started shaking.

And when the bear added his strength, the rock toppled over.

They rushed out of the cave.

Then they decided to go as fast as the wind, not as fast as thought, because they would get killed.

When the boy saw that his puppies weren't coming, he started climbing down, because the *zmeu* was becoming more insistent.

But then he saw his puppies coming as fast as

a hurricane, so he retrieved his courage and climbed back up.

The *zmeu*, when he saw the puppies, transformed himself into an old log.

"What do you command, master?" asked the puppies.

"Can you see that old log?" the boy said.

"We can see it."

"Rip it to pieces. Shake it, tear it apart, devour all of it, apart from the heart and the liver."

They started on the old log, tore it apart, and turned it to dust.

Within moments, there was nothing left of the log other than the *zmeu*'s heart and liver.

Climbing down from the tree, the boy took the *zmeu*'s heart and liver and returned home with his puppies.

He asked his sister to put the meat on the fire, to roast it.

After the meat started browning, the boy took it from his sister's hand.

He tenderized it on all sides and put salt on it.

He then put it on the fire again and left it to roast until the juices came out.

Then he took the roast in his hand, and told his sister:

"Sister, look at me, because since I have known you, I have never seen your eyes."

She looked at him.

He threw the roast in her eyes and blinded her.

"To retrieve your eyesight, you need to cry until you fill nine barrels with your tears," he told her. "Once you have started on the ninth, I will come back and help."

He set off playing his pipes with his puppies in tow, leaving his sister to atone for her sins.

And he went, and kept going, until he came out of that terrible forest and reached a village.

As he felt thirsty, he knocked on the door of one of the houses and asked for some water.

An old woman came out of the house:

"I don't have any to give you, my dear," she said, "because we only have one well. In it lives a large dragon. He only lets someone have water if they give him a human head in return."

"Bring a bucket," said the lad, "and I will go fetch water."

He took the bucket and went to the well.

He drew water and drank, then brought the old woman the bucket full.

As soon as the old woman saw it, she drank the whole bucket, because she was dying of thirst.

She asked him to bring another one, and when he brought it to her, he drank that one as well.

"May God bless you, my dear lad," the old woman said. "I had forgotten what water tasted like, and it felt as if I'd lost my soul. I was about to die from thirst. Bring me another one, and may you find blessings in the other world."

The lad went to the well to get another bucket of water.

When he got to the well, he found a beautiful girl next to it, crying her eyes out.

"Why are you crying, young girl?" he asked her.

"How would I not cry, when I am about to die?"

"Why do you think you are about to die?"

"You know that in this well there is a large snake-like dragon which is haunting mankind?"

"I have heard about it, but I have never seen it. I am from elsewhere, and have only just arrived here. But if what you are saying is true, why are you staying here, to be eaten by the dragon? Don't you have a home to go to?"

"I do have a home. But over here, the custom is that everyone has to give a head to this insatiable dragon, to let them take water from the well, because this is the only well in this place. And now it is our turn to give a person to be eaten by this beast. And dad only has me. He is the king of this place, and he has sacrificed me to do his bit."

The lad felt pity for her.

"Don't worry," the lad said, "you won't get eaten by the dragon, you're with me."

"Save yourself," said the girl. "There is no point in wasting two innocent lives. How many young men like you, even bigger and stronger than you, have been killed by this blasted beast."

"Let me try. If the dragon kills me as well, that's okay. No one will miss me, apart from my puppies. What signs does the dragon give when it is coming out?"

"The well begins to roar."

"Fine. Let me rest and, when you hear the roar, wake me up. But don't look through my quiver of arrows."

He put his head in the girl's lap and fell asleep straight away, as if someone had hit him on the head.

The girl could not contain her curiosity and looked through his quiver of arrows.

While looking, she lost one of the arrows.

As the well started roaring, she was too scared to wake him up, in case he would tell her off for losing the arrow.

She started to cry bitterly, to melt your heart.

A tear fell on his cheek and he jumped up.

"What was it that fell on my cheek?" he asked.

"One of my tears," the girl replied. "The well started to roar."

The lad took his bow and went to the entry of the well.

"Come out, cursed beast!" he shouted.

"What do you want with me, lad?" the dragon asked. "I let you get as much water as you wanted."

"I want to fight you and kill you."

"I don't have anything against you," the dragon said. "Go mind your own business. I have work to do, based on the agreement I have with the people of this place."

The lad pulled on his bow and as the arrow flew, he cut off one of the dragon's tongues, of which there were nine.

The dragon came out of the well, his remaining tongues playing in his maw as fast as lightning, and they fought.

The dragon was throwing his tongues towards the boy, to devour him.

The lad threw another arrow, took out another tongue, and another, and another, until he had taken out eight tongues.

When he was about to put in a ninth arrow, he couldn't find it, so he grabbed a pin out of the girl's hair, put it in the bow, and with it took out the dragon's ninth tongue.

Blood came gushing out of the beast, dark, gloomy, and foul-smelling.

The dragon thrashed about for a while, then fell down dead.

The boy asked the girl for a handkerchief, placed the tongues in it and set off playing his pipes, with the puppies after him.

The girl called after him.

When she saw he wasn't coming back, she realized that she missed him and she collapsed crying.

Meanwhile, the king's cook went to the well to get some water.

When he reached the fountain, he was shocked to find the dragon dead in a pool of blood.

He was also surprised to find the girl unharmed, as he knew she had been sent to the well as a sacrifice to the dragon.

Then, regaining his wits, he covered himself in the dragon's blood from head to toe, rushed back to the king, and told him that he had done a great deed.

He had killed the dragon who had been haunting his kingdom and had saved the king's daughter from death.

The king didn't quite believe what his cook was telling him, but changed his mind when the cook brought the girl back unharmed.

The girl said that another man had killed the dragon, but the cook was adamant that it was he who had done the brave deed.

He also asked the king for his daughter's hand in marriage, as a reward for the great danger he had faced to save her.

The king had promised a while back that if there was anyone brave enough to rescue his daughter from the dragon, he would get the girl's hand in marriage.

The girl didn't want to marry the cook.

She looked towards where the lad had left with his puppies, saw him, and pointed him out to her dad.

The king sent messengers to tell the lad the king wanted to speak to him.

The lad was initially reluctant to go before the king, as he had never set foot in a royal palace before and didn't know how to behave.

But the messengers insisted, and he eventually agreed to come with them to the king.

"Young lad," the king said, "was it you who rescued my daughter from death?"

"Yes it was, your highness."

"He is lying, your highness," said the cook.

"Can you prove to us it was you who killed that wretched beast?" the king asked.

"The beast's tongues bear witness to this," said the lad.

Then he took out his handkerchief and showed him the tongues.

"That is my handkerchief," the girl said. "I gave it to him to put the tongues inside it."

The cook took fright when he saw the tongues.

The king sent for the head of the dragon.

And when he looked inside the maw, everybody saw that the dragon's tongues were missing.

The king decided that the lad who had killed the dragon would marry his daughter.

He also ordered for the cook to be tied to the tails of two young horses, which he set off and the horses tore the man in half.

Then they had a great big wedding.

As the young man saw that things were going well for him, he remembered his sister's betrayal.

He decided to look for her and release her from her sin.

He set off on his journey, his puppies after him.

He found his sister crying away her sins, having already filled eight barrels with her tears.

He helped her with the ninth, until this one was full as well.

Then she washed her cheeks and eyes with this mixing of tears, and her eyesight returned.

Yet she was still bearing resentment towards him.

When daylight came, she said:

"Brother, put your head in my lap, the way you used to do when we were little, and take a nap. It will remind us of our childhood."

"You're right, sister. Let's leave our troubles behind."

He put his head in her lap and fell asleep.

His sister took out one of the *zmeu*'s bones, which she had found and kept, and stuck it inside her brother's skull.

The boy died straight away.

She put his body inside a barrel and threw it down the river.

As soon as the puppies sensed that their master had died, they wailed so pitifully, it would melt your heart.

The wolf started to run with his nose in the air in all directions until he found the area where the barrel was floating.

They all followed the barrel along the edge of the river until the water brought the barrel towards the shore.

The bear kept watch until it felt right, then he jumped into the water, took hold of the barrel, dragged it onto dry land, and broke it with his paw.

They took out their master's body from the barrel and started to grieve him.

As they were grieving, a magpie came by.

While playing around and wagging her tail, she sang:

"Cheep, cheep, you have to catch a magpie, but not me, but one like me. To break her neck, pour three drops of blood on the body you are grieving, and it will return to life."

The fox, being a trickster, said to her:

"What are you saying? I can't hear. Come closer and tell us again, so we can hear properly."

The magpie came closer.

When she was about to sing a second time, the fox snatched her up.

And breaking the magpie's neck, they put three drops of blood over their master and he came back to life.

"Phew, that was a deep sleep," he said.

"You would have slept longer, if it hadn't been for us."

The boy felt a stabbing pain behind his ear.

The bear looked, and seeing the *zmeu* bone, he sucked on it until it came out of the boy's skull.

Then he started licking the wound until it closed and healed.

The lad washed his eyes, took his pipes and left with the puppies after him.

He returned to his wife, who was anxiously waiting for him, and asked some royal servants to bring in his sister.

And calling in the big judges, he asked for judgement to be passed between him and his sister.

The judges decided that she should be put to death.

Then the king came down from his throne and asked his son-in-law to take his place, because he saw that the young man was brave and fair, like a good king should be.

And I jumped into a saddle and told you the story thus.

This tale's original title is 'Copiii vaduvului si iepurele, vulpea, lupul si ursul', which translates as 'The widower's children and the rabbit, the fox, the wolf and the bear'.

I was delighted to find and translate a tale that starts in such a similar way to *Hansel and Gretel*, yet follows such a different trajectory once the story gets going.

I was also delighted and surprised to find a love story between a human girl and a male *zmeu* in this tale, even if it does not have a happy-ever-after ending.

The *zmeu*, in case you are not familiar with Romanian folklore, is a monster-like creature that appears in many Romanian fairy tales, legends, and myths.

There is no formal consensus over what a *zmeu* looks like, but based on what happens in the stories, we can tell that the *zmeu* shares many human-like features.

He has arms and legs, as well as the ability to ride a horse and use weapons.

The monster-like features include having a tail as well as being bigger and stronger than humans.

In most stories, the behavior of the *zmeu* in relation to humans follows a rather predictable pattern.

The hero's quest is usually set in motion by the *zmeu* kidnapping a beautiful young maiden, whom the hero has to rescue from the *zmeu*.

The *zmeu* is often helped by his mother, who usually has a whole range of magic powers and chases after the hero or attempts to outwit him once her son has been defeated.

In *The Rabbit, the Fox, the Wolf, and the Bear*, we find an unusual scenario: the girl and the *zmeu* fall in love with one another.

There is no pressure from the part of the *zmeu* over the girl, nor is his mother mentioned as an additional villainous character in the story.

It is interesting that as this love story unfolds, the girl turns into a villain herself, suggesting perhaps that no good thing comes from falling in love with a *zmeu*.

Yet even the possibility of such a romance between a human and a *zmeu* in this story is intriguing.

Aside from the *zmeu*, another fantastic creature you encountered in this story is a dragon.

The dragon in this story is a *balaur*, which is the Romanian version of this type of creature.

I chose not to use the Romanian term, as depictions of the *balaur* show a creature that any Western readers would easily recognize as a dragon.

However, it is worth noting that in some Romanian stories, the term *balaur* can occasionally refer to any monster-like creature, not just dragons.

One important change I made in translating this story relates to the ethnic identity of the impostor, who claims he was the one who had slain the dragon.

In the original version, the impostor is

referred to as a Gypsy (a pejorative term for a member of the Rroma ethnic group).

Unfortunately, this choice of ethnicity is a common feature of many of the villains in the stories collected by Petre Ispirescu.

As much as I love these stories, this particular aspect saddens me.

I imagine it must be difficult for Rroma people reading these stories to see themselves portrayed in this way.

In translating and adapting these stories, I made the choice to take out this racist element of the stories wherever I encountered it.

As a translator, I have to be faithful to the original material, but not if doing so would perpetuate prejudice and discrimination.

As such, I felt it was my duty to remove the racist undertones from this story.

Fortunately, this was an easy change to make in terms of the logic of the narrative.

As the ethnic aspect was not a crucial part of the story, I simply described impostor in terms of their profession (a cook) instead of referring to them in terms of their ethnic identity.

THE MAGIC TREE

There was once a great king who was praised by his entire kingdom, because he was a good man.

He had peace and abundance in his kingdom.

All the other kings, his neighbors, were envious of him.

He wasn't satisfied with words.

He would go for himself to see with his own eyes how things are going in his kingdom.

He knew everything, saw everything, and would fix things so they went well.

Only one thing was troubling him.

In the middle of his garden was a tree, so tall you couldn't see its peak.

He didn't know how tall that tree was, because nobody had dared climb it.

The trunk was smooth and would slide like ice.

Eventually, he decided to find out more about this tree.

He sent out messengers through his entire country to let everyone know that the first man who will succeed in climbing that tree will receive half his kingdom and his daughter's hand in marriage.

Not long passed and he gathered a large crowd of young men who wanted to climb the tree.

Day after day, the men tried, but none of them could climb that tree.

Those who succeeded in reaching higher than the others couldn't find any branch to hang on to, and had to climb down again.

On the ninth day towards evening, three shepherds happened to pass by.

They saw the crowd of people at the king's court and stopped to have a look.

One of the king's servants invited them to come in.

After the servant told them why the crowd

had gathered, and what the one who will succeed will receive, the shepherds went into the garden.

They didn't want people to think they're simply busy-bodies, so the older one among them started to climb.

He climbed and climbed, but he could not find any branch and had to climb down again.

The same thing happened to the middle one.

The youngest one wanted to try as well, but the older two tried to stop him.

He was a bit smaller than the other two, but he was adamant that he wanted to try, and eventually his companions relented.

After looking at the tree from all sides, the young shepherd had the idea of asking for nine loafs of bread, nine glasses of wine, and nine planks of wood.

The king ordered for these to be brought straight away and the shepherd put them in his bag.

Then he spit into his hands, said a short prayer, and started climbing.

He crossed his arms and legs around the tree's trunk and slowly, slowly, he started making progress.

There were many people underneath the

tree watching him, but he didn't lose courage, and kept on climbing.

Not long passed and the people down below could no longer see him.

The young man was climbing like a hero.

When the wind started blowing, he took out one of the wooden planks, stuck it well into the tree and sat on it to rest a little.

He then took out a loaf of bread and ate it, then poured himself a glass of wine, which he drank.

After renewing his strengths, he climbed some more, but with greater difficulty, because the wind was weakening his strength.

Then he took out another plank of wood, had another rest, ate another loaf of bread, drank another glass of wine, and again started to climb.

He kept doing this until he had finished all the food he had with him.

After reaching a certain height, he was able to climb more easily, because he was able to find branches to hold on to.

He climbed and climbed, until he came close to the top of the tree.

Suddenly, as he reached that point, a whole

new land opened up before him, which took him by surprise.

He found himself in a large field, so big you couldn't see its end.

The trees looked different from the land he came from, even the weeds looked different from the ones he knew.

He looked to see if there were any other human beings in that place, but he could not see anybody.

What to do? Where to go?

He wanted to turn back, but he couldn't find the place from which he had come.

It started getting darker, and he didn't know where to go.

He walked and walked, until he saw in the distance a sort of chimney.

As he had no other choice, he walked in that direction.

That was the land of the Ghesperita, who suddenly appeared before him.

"Who are you who dared to tread on my land?" said the Ghesperita.

"I am called Piciu," the shepherd said.

He was so scared, as if the veil had suddenly

lifted from his eyes, and his sins had brought him to this place.

"You see this field?" said the Ghesperita. "Tonight you will plow it, sow it, harvest the grains, and grind them. Then you will make me an oven. Tomorrow, when I get up, you will have warm bread ready for me to eat, if you want to escape with your soul."

Then the Ghesperita went away to sleep.

Piciu started to cry with such sorrow, your heart would melt from pity.

He could see that what she had asked for was impossible to accomplish.

He was crying and wailing, waiting for his death.

Suddenly, a beautiful girl appeared before him.

She was so beautiful that he forgot all his troubles while looking at her.

"Why are you crying, boy?" she asked.

"How would I not cry," Piciu replied, as if he had just awoken from a dream.

Then he told her what the Ghesperita had asked for.

"I would do it," he said, "if it was possible to accomplish what she asked, but it isn't possible.

That's why I was crying when you came. Though I don't know why, but since seeing you, I seem to have gotten some courage."

"No need to cry, everything will get done. Wait here, I will return."

After a little while, she returned holding a whip.

She cracked the whip three times and a group of devils appeared.

"What is your wish, mistress?" the devils asked.

"I want you to plow the field you are seeing," she said. "I also want you to sow it, harvest it, grind the grains, and before daybreak I want there to be warm bread in the oven you will build this very night. Go and set to work."

Then she turned towards Piciu and said:

"Now go to sleep, the task you have been given will get done."

"I don't want to go to sleep before I find out who you are, whom God has sent to help me."

"Well lad, may God not let other girls go through what I have been through. The Ghesperita had a son. He was just as evil and ugly as her. I don't know how he saw me in my parents' garden, because I am from the other place, where you are from, and he fancied me. I had parents and a big brother who had become famous around the world for his skills as an archer. One day, while I was feeding the birds in the garden, I suddenly felt myself grabbed by the armpits and pulled up. I screamed so loudly, everyone heard. It turns out Ghesperita's son had grabbed me and was climbing up with me. As soon as my brother heard, he came outside with his bow in his hand and aimed. When he released the arrow, he hit Ghesperita's son straight in the ribs. My kidnapper died, but before he did, he handed me over to his mother who was waiting on this side. Out of anger for having lost her son, she kept me in this place. Otherwise I am not living badly, but when I remember my parents and my brother, I am overcome by homesickness. But how did you get here?"

Piciu told her how he had climbed the tree.

Afterwards, he found himself a place where he could rest, and went to sleep.

At daybreak, Piciu got up, went to the field, and was stunned by what he saw.

The entire field had been harvested, with only a few strands of straw left at the edge of the field.

At the other edge, an enormous oven was still going and loaves of bread, already baked, were piled up next to the oven.

While he was still marveling at all that had been accomplished overnight, he saw the Ghesperita coming towards him so fast the earth was shaking.

"Give me something to eat, I am famished," she said.

Piciu started to throw one loaf of bread at a time into her mouth and she swallowed them without chewing, until all the loaves were gone.

"You have been lucky," the Ghesperita said to Piciu. "Before daybreak tomorrow, I want you to make me a vineyard on that hill there. Plant these vine seedlings, grow them into grapes, harvest them, stamp on them, and put the wine in the barrels, for me to drink. If not, I will eat you like a sparrow chick."

She left, and Piciu started crying with such sorrow, even the wood and the stones were melting from pity.

The girl reappeared and asked him why he was crying.

He told her everything the Ghesperita had ordered him to do.

The girl waited until the Ghesperita had gone to sleep and once again brought out the whip, cracked it three times, and the devils came as numerous as leaves of grass.

She ordered them what to do, then turned to Piciu and said:

"Now you can relax and stop worrying, the task will get done."

When Piciu got up at daybreak, his eyes were mesmerized by what he saw.

The entire hill was covered by a large vineyard which had been harvested.

The barrels were full.

The utensils used to make the wine had been cleaned and put away.

While he was marveling at this miracle, he saw the Ghesperita coming towards him like a storm.

"Give me the wine," she said in a loud voice that would freeze you to death.

Piciu pulled a cork from one of the barrels and Ghesperita put her mouth at the opening of the barrel and started drinking.

After she finished the barrel, he pulled a cork from another barrel, then another, until all the barrels were empty.

"Oh, you rascal," she said. "Luck has served you again, otherwise I would have eaten you raw. Before tomorrow, I want to find a blue rabbit, cooked. You must catch it from the thousands of rabbits that are in that forest. The rabbit has to be neither overcooked, nor too raw. Understood? If not, you will not live to see another day."

As soon as she said this, she went away like a storm.

When he heard this latest order and the threat she had made, Piciu's heart stopped and he was about to die.

But the girl appeared and gave him courage.

"There is no reason to despair," she told him. "Leave things be, you have worked yourself up too much. I have helped you with two fairly difficult things, and yet this third time you have lost your courage, and it's as if you want to take your own life. Didn't I tell you I'm around? And while I am alive, you don't need to worry about anything."

"Yes, you have said all this to me," he said. "But this time, I don't know how, I don't know why, you seem to have come later than the other times. Look, the sun has set, and you have only just appeared."

"It's because," she said, "the Ghesperita has guessed that I am helping you, and has hidden the whip. Whereas before she was keeping it underneath her head, now she has fallen asleep holding it in her arms. Luckily, the wine got to her. I had to wait for her to fall into deep sleep, otherwise I could not have taken it."

She taught him what he had to do, then she cracked the whip and transformed into a fire-eating steed.

They went into the forest and started to sound the horn, to make all the beasts come out into the field.

When she thought enough time had passed for Piciu to catch a blue rabbit, she went to find him.

But instead of him having accomplished the task, she found him sleeping.

"I am running around doing everything for you," she said as she woke him up, "and you are sleeping like a log. All the beasts have already come out of the forest. I don't know if there will be any left now."

"I don't know what blasted tiredness has come over me. My body was heavy, my hands were weak and my eyes were closing despite myself. I have tried to keep myself awake for as long as I could, have strived to remain upright, but all my efforts were in vain."

"Now there's no other option," the girl said, "than to do it the hard way. I will wander through all the corners of the forest sounding the horn. As soon as you see a rabbit, you have to catch it, otherwise we are both lost."

He set off and wandered through the forest again and again.

Not a single beast was left.

He ran across and sideways, in a deep hollow, he found a blue rabbit.

As soon as he saw the boy, the rabbit started sprinting, and the boy ran after him.

Piciu was close to losing him.

When the rabbit jumped, Piciu, from where he was kneeling with his chest open, suddenly jumped to his feet.

The rabbit, frightened, jumped straight onto Piciu's chest.

Piciu pulled up his chest, put his hand inside and caught the rabbit.

After teaching him what to do next, the girl took the whip and waited for him a distance away.

Piciu skinned the rabbit, made a big fire, and fried the meat.

Once the meat was ready, he took it out of the fire, and grabbed the rabbit by his hind legs.

As it was nearly daybreak, he went into the hut where Ghesperita was sleeping and hit her over the eyes with the hot rabbit.

Then he ran towards the girl, who was waiting for him.

The girl, still in the shape of a steed, let Piciu ride her.

They ran, and ran, to escape Ghesperita's fury.

Ghesperita woke up blind from the rabbit that had been thrust into her eyes.

She sent her husband to catch them and bring them back live and unharmed, so she could punish them.

Ghesperita's husband went after them, riding a better horse, which was running like the wind.

"Look behind," the girl said, as Gesperita's husband was about to reach them, "and tell me what you see, because my eyes have started watering."

"I see a darkness coming after us like the wind."

Then the girl, after teaching him what to do, transformed into some straw mounds with corn, along which some hens were pecking away at the straw.

And Piciu transformed into an old man with a hunchback.

As soon as Ghesperita's husband got there, he went to the old man:

"Can you hear me, old man?" he asked.

Piciu was looking down, pretending he can't see or hear him, and kept chasing the hens away from the straw.

"Go away, you blasted one," he was saying.

"Old man," Ghesperita's husband said, shaking him, "did you see a boy and a girl passing through here?"

"I didn't see," he replied, "shoo!...I saw and I didn't see...shoo! May the one who has you eat you raw."

He was talking and not looking him in the face.

When Ghesperita's husband saw he couldn't find out anything from the old man, he went back to his wife and told her he wasn't able to find them.

"Go," the Ghesperita said with fury, "and

bring them back however way, I will suck them up in a go."

The girl, as soon as she saw Ghesperita's husband resuming the chase, transformed again into a horse.

With Piciu riding her, she ran and kept running.

"Look behind you," she told him as she felt Ghesperita's husband approaching, "because I have started to lose my sight. A mist has settled over my eyes. Tell me what you see."

"A darkness is following us once more, coming as fast as thought."

The girl cracked the whip and turned into an old church, with moss growing on her three fingers, and the stone threshold all worn out.

She turned Piciu into an old monk, so old you'd need sticks to keep his eyelids open.

The monk was reading and nodding his head.

As soon as Ghesperita's husband reached the church, he got off the horse and went into the church.

"Have you seen a boy and a girl passing by here, old monk?" he asked, when he saw the monk.

Piciu wasn't taking his eyes off the book.

He was reading and praying.

In the end, seeing he wasn't getting any peace, he said:

"I saw, I didn't see. Hallelujah...Beauty, youth, hallelujah...God and my thought. Hallelujah....Over here trouble you won't see. Hallelujah..."

When he saw he wasn't getting anywhere with the monk, Ghesperita's husband returned home.

"I didn't come across any boy," he said.

"Have you come across anything on your way?" Ghesperita asked.

"Yes, I came across an old church with the moss three feet deep and a monk inside, so old he had to pull his eyelids up with sticks and speaking nonsense."

"That was them, you idiot," Ghesperita said. "Why didn't you grab them?"

She was so full of anger and hatred, she couldn't sit still, so she decided to go after them herself.

"Look behind you," the girl said, "and tell me what you see. I am getting so hot I can't go on any more."

"A flame and a fire are coming towards us," he said.

The girl cracked the whip and turned herself into a large deep lake, and Piciu became a beautiful male duck.

As soon as the Ghesperita got there, she told the duck, who was swimming in the middle of the lake:

"Duckling, duckling, come towards the edge so I can ask you something."

"Ask away," the duckling said, "I can hear you from here."

"Come over, or I'll suck you up water and all."

"You won't do that, because you will burst, when you'll suck up the water."

Ghesperita couldn't contain her anger and started drinking the lake with one gulp.

She drank and drank, but couldn't reach the duck, and burst into pieces.

The girl turned to her own self again, cracked the whip in four directions and all the lands of the Ghesperita became a pomegranate seed.

They found themselves back in the king's garden, where Piciu had started his journey.

The tree he had climbed had completely vanished.

As soon as the king and the king's servants saw them, they treated them as honored guests.

They recognized the girl as being the daughter of a neighboring king, and sent word to her father of her return.

The king, wanting to keep his word, said to Piciu:

"My son, the soul travels the same way as one's words. So I am ready keep the promise I made when you started climbing the tree."

"Enlightened king," Piciu said, pointing to his chest, "I too have something there. But fairness requires that I share the goods on this earth with the one with whom I have shared the bad times. If the girl you are seeing before you wasn't there, I would have long been on the other side."

"Fine, son," the king said. "If this is how it is, I am giving a part of my kingdom to you, for the bravery you have shown. I will be your godfather, and the marriage to the girl you have chosen for yourself will be in a few days time."

Just then the other king appeared, the girl's father, with his son, a brave and handsome young man.

When he heard what the king had decided, he said:

"I too will give a part of my kingdom to this young lad, who has helped my daughter come back."

As the girl's brother and the daughter of the king with the tall tree fell in love with one another, they made two weddings at the same time.

The rejoicing at their weddings was beyond words.

After that, everyone went their way, living in happiness even today, if they haven't yet died.

And I jumped into a saddle and told you the story thus.

TRANSLATOR'S NOTE (THE MAGIC TREE)

The original title of this tale is 'Piciul ciobanasul si copacul fara capatai', which translates as 'Piciul the young shepherd and the tree without end'.

On a personal level, this story was one of my favorites, as it contains so many delightful elements.

The adventure in this tale arises out of a story trope that comes up often in the tales collected by Petre Ispirescu, that of a king who is intrigued by one of the trees in his garden and requires the help of a young male hero to satiate his curiosity.

The female love interest in this tale is no damsel in distress, she is a strong and courageous woman with magic powers.

Uncharacteristically for Petre Ispirescu's

tales, it is she who rescues the male lead, rather than the other way around.

The shapeshifting in this tale is also more extensive than in most tales.

The characters do not just shapeshift into animals, birds, or insects, as is usually the case in most fairy tales.

They have the ability to shapeshift into buildings or places as well, if the need arises.

THE GOLDEN CHILDREN

Once upon a time, there was a wealthy young man who had travelled the world and was on his way back to his estate.

While going through a field, he saw three girls working.

He was walking by, minding his own business, until something the girls said caught his attention.

He returned to the girls and asked them:

"Girls, what were you saying?"

"If the young man who is passing by would marry me," the eldest girl said, "I would clothe all his servants with a spindle".

"If the young man who is passing by would

marry me," the middle girl said, "I would feed all his servants with one loaf of bread."

"If the young man who is passing by would marry me," the youngest of the girls said, "I would birth him two children made entirely of gold."

The young man spent some time thinking about what they had said.

After changing his mind several times, he said to the youngest of the girls:

"I liked your words better than those of your sisters. I would like to marry you, just as long as you keep your word."

The girl blushed like a rose.

Then, after they talked for a little while, she held out her hand and said:

"If you are the one destined for me, I will not leave you, nor you me, no matter who tries to keep us apart."

The young man took the girl to his estate, where he owned some palaces more beautiful than she'd ever laid her eyes on.

Their wedding lasted a long time and was talked about in foreign lands.

Not long passed and the girl became pregnant.

When the young man heard this, he was overcome with joy.

He hired a servant girl to help out his new wife with whatever she needed.

The servant, as soon as she met the new bride, started harboring dark thoughts against her.

When the girl went into labor, the young man was away on a business trip.

The girl asked the servant to call the midwife, but the servant brought her mother instead.

When she came, the servant's mother said:

"The custom around here is to birth by going into the attic while giving birth. I will be down-stairs, holding the crib."

"If this is how it is around here, let's do it that way," the girl said.

She was pure at heart and did not realize that someone could harbor dark thoughts against her.

She went into the attic and gave birth, as she had promised, to two babies covered in gold.

The babies fell into the crib the servant's mother was holding underneath the entrance to the attic.

As soon as she saw the pretty babies, the servant went to bury them in the stable dung.

She replaced the babies with two puppies that had been born that same day.

Then the servant's mother showed the puppies to the girl and told her that this is what she had birthed.

"How is that possible?" the girl said, and she started arguing with the servant's mother.

Meanwhile, the young man arrived home.

The servant welcomed him and showed him the crib with the two puppies.

"Look what your wife has birthed. Just as well God has inspired you to bring in a faithful servant such as me, to be around her. Otherwise, who knows how she would have tried to fool you, and laugh behind your back."

The young man was furious when he saw the puppies, and regarded this as an insult.

To punish his wife, he divorced her, married the servant, and made his former wife become her new servant.

The poor woman could see how unfairly she had been treated.

But not having any choice, she kept quiet and put up with her new life.

She put her faith in God that He will show her mercy, and that she will eventually be able to provide proof of her innocence.

Some time passed, and two apple trees grew out of the dung where the two children had been buried.

The bark of those trees was covered in gold.

Even at night, the two trees shone as brightly as the sun.

They were growing as fast in a day as if a year had passed by, and they soon became fully-fledged trees.

The new wife became worried, seeing the beauty of these trees.

"Cut down those two apple trees that are growing next to the stables," she told her husband. "I would like to turn them into boards for our bed, because we are missing a couple."

"Why would I cut down those beautiful apple trees? Don't you see they are unlike any other? Nobody else owns such beautiful trees."

"If you don't cut down those trees, I will leave you".

The young man cut down the apples trees and turned them into boards for the bed.

During the night, the wife heard the boards talking to one another.

"Sister," one of the boards was saying, because the children were a boy and a girl. "Sister," said the boy, "are you having it heavy?"

"Heavy," said the girl, "because the deceitful one is on me. Is it heavy for you?"

"No, it's not heavy," said the boy, "because it's Dad who is lying on me."

The wife realized that the talking of the boards could be her undoing, if her husband heard them, and she couldn't sleep until morning.

"Husband," she said to him in the morning, "these new boards have given me nightmares. You must cut them up."

"How am I to cut such beautiful boards?"

"I don't know. But if you don't cut them, I will go off and kill myself."

To get rid of her nagging, the husband cut down the boards and turned them into firewood, which the wife burned in the fireplace.

But two splinters snuck out through the chimney and fell into the garden.

Two basil plants grew where those splinters had fallen.

One of the little lambs ate the basil, and his wool turned golden.

The little lamb became so beautiful, there wasn't any other lamb like that in the entire world.

The wife was livid when she saw the lamb, because she understood that this was not good for her.

Some time passed.

One day, when she saw her husband in a good mood, she told him:

"How I'd eat meat from that golden lamb of ours!"

"How can you think of such a thing? I like that lamb," the husband said.

When the wife saw that this time she couldn't nag him into it, she turned to cunning and made herself ill.

She tortured her husband a whole week, complaining about her illness.

Then, one night, she pretended to wake up with a jolt.

When her husband asked her what had happened, she said:

"I dreamt that a witch doctor had come and

told me that the only way for me to get well is if you kill that lamb of ours, so I can eat its meat."

"What are you talking about?" the man asked. "Where in the world have you seen such a beautiful lamb? Better to call a healer to give you cures to get you well again."

"This is my cure," she said. "You either kill that lamb so I can eat its meat, or I will die."

Not having any choice, the husband killed the lamb and gave it to the cook to turn it into food.

The wife went to the kitchen and ordered how the lamb should be cooked so that nothing would remain of it.

She sent one of her faithful servants to the river with the entrails.

She instructed this servant to wash the entrails, to count them all up, and then to bring them back.

She also told the servant she will pay with her life if she loses the tiniest bit.

While washing them in the river, the servant broke off one of the ends by mistake.

She panicked and threw it down the river.

Then she returned home with all the entrails,

apart from the missing bit, which her mistress did not notice.

The next day, the former wife, the one who had birthed the two children, went to the river with a pitcher to get some water.

When she arrived, she saw two little children on a mound, playing with golden apples.

The children and the apples were so golden, they were making the earth shine.

She stayed there until evening looking at them, because she sensed they might be her children.

When she returned home, her mistress beat her up.

"Stop beating me, mistress," the woman said. "What my eyes have seen, you can look at for an entire week and not get enough."

When the wife heard this, she went to see, and indeed she stood there looking at the children as if lost in a trance.

How could she leave such unseen beauty behind?

The children were playing with such joy, just looking at them made you feel lucky to be alive.

The children's mother came and woke her up from the daze she had fallen into:

"See, mistress? I was telling you that you cannot have enough of such beauty, no matter how long you looked."

Meanwhile, more and more people were coming to look at the children, but they did not know how to get them to come off that little mound of earth in the middle of the river and swim to shore.

Among the onlookers was an old woman, wiser than the rest, who did not have children of her own and decided to adopt them.

She went home and returned with a small fork and staff.

With these she went to the edge of the river, showed them to the children, and called them to her with a warm voice.

As soon as the children saw these tools, they immediately swam towards the old woman.

The girl grabbed the fork, and the boy the staff.

The old woman took the children with her, got them dressed, and settled them in her home.

Not long passed and the husband gathered all the boys and girls from the village to tell stories in a circle.

The old woman went too, with the two children.

The husband happened to be in a good mood that day.

"You know what?" he said. "Children, instead of telling stories about all sorts of nothings, how about you each tell me a story about your own life."

All received the young man's invite in good spirit.

Everyone had a story to tell about their life.

Then it was the turn of the old woman's children to tell their story.

"Well, Sir, what shall we tell you?" they said. "We don't know any stories."

"Of course you do. Tell me whatever story you know."

Then the boy started:

"There were once three girls who were working in a field. A wealthy young man passed by, and the elder of the girls said:

'If the young man passing by marries me, I will clothe all his servants with a spindle.'

The middle girl said: 'If the young man passing by picks me, I will feed all his servants with a loaf of bread.'

The youngest girl said: 'If he picks me, I will birth him two children made entirely of gold.'

The young man took the youngest girl as his wife, and hired a servant girl to help her day-to-day.

Some time passed, and the wife became pregnant.

When she was about to give birth, the young man wasn't home.

The wife asked her servant to bring her the midwife, but the servant brought in her own mother.

The mother said that it's the custom, in that part of the world, that the ladies give birth by going into the attic and the midwife to be at the entry into the attic with the crib.

The girl did not realize this was a trap.

She went into the attic and gave birth to two children made entirely of gold.

The servant buried the babies in the stable dung and replaced them with two puppies that had recently been birthed.

She showed the puppies to the husband, telling him that this is what his wife had birthed.

The young man was angry at his wife and decided to punish her.

He divorced her and married the servant, while making his former wife work as a servant for his new wife.

From the dung, two apple trees grew, with golden bark.

The new wife, as soon as she saw the trees, nagged her husband to cut them down and turn them into boards for their bed.

During the night, she heard the boards speaking to one another.

The board underneath her husband said: 'Are you feeling heavy?'

'Yes,' the other board replied, 'the impostor is lying on me. Is it heavy for you?'

'No, because Dad is lying on me.'

Then the wife nagged her husband to cut up the boards and turn them into firewood.

She set fire to the wood, but two splinters jumped through the chimney and fell into the garden.

From these splinters, two basil bushes grew.

One of the little lambs ate the basil and his wool became golden.

When the wife noticed this, she pretended to be ill and asked her husband to kill the lamb so she could eat its meat in order to regain her health.

The husband resisted her nagging, but she persisted.

To escape her nagging, he eventually killed the lamb.

The wife sent one of her servants with the lamb's entrails, to wash them at the river.

While the servant washed them, a tiny bit broke off, and went floating down the river.

The wife did not notice that a bit had gone missing.

The bit stopped on a shore, and that's where we came from.

From there an old woman took us and brought us into her home, where she is bringing us up as her children. The master of this estate has ordered a story circle, and we came by, and here we are, as whole as the day we were born."

All those who were present were thunder-struck by the boy's tale.

Then the boy finished his story saying:

"And if you don't believe me, look and take faith."

The boy and the girl took off their clothes.

Their skin shone so brightly that nobody could take their eyes off them.

Their father took them into his arms, and as soon as he did, they got glued to his heart, giving him final proof that they were his children.

Their mother came as well and took them to her bosom.

They all cried of happiness that God had brought them back together.

Then the father of the children, furious with his wife's deception, ordered that two untrained horses be brought from the stables.

Then he tied his deceitful wife to the tails of the horses, together with a sack of nuts, and released the horses into the world.

Where a nut would fall, a piece of her flesh would fall as well, until there was nothing left of her but dust.

And I jumped into a saddle and told you the story thus.

TRANSLATOR'S NOTE (THE GOLDEN CHILDREN)

The original title of this story is 'Insira-te margar-itar', which broadly translates as 'One pearl after another'.

The title makes reference to a rhyme the boy uses repeatedly while telling the story of how he and his sister survived the many attempts on their life.

While translating this tale, I initially attempted to include this rhyme, but its power was lost in translation.

As a result, I chose to leave the rhyme out, as doing so served the story better.

Another important change I made was that I did not mention the ethnic identity of the deceitful wife, who in the original version is referred to as a Gypsy (a pejorative term used to describe members of the Rroma ethnic group).

This is a problem I have already discussed in the Translator's Note relating to *The Rabbit, the Fox, the Wolf, and the Bear*.

As previously mentioned, in translating and adapting these stories, I made the choice to take out any racist elements wherever I encountered them.

As a translator, I have to be faithful to the original material, but not if doing so would perpetuate prejudice and discrimination.

As such, I felt it was my duty to remove the racist undertones from this story, and simply referred to the character in terms of her role as a servant.

I have also changed the way I referred to the young man in this story, the father of the two children.

In the original version, he is described throughout the tale as the 'son of a *boiar*'.

The term *boiar* points to a person of high status in the Romanian feudal system.

This term does not have an exact translation in the English language.

However, whenever this term has come up in

other stories, I have translated it as 'aristocrat', as that is the closest equivalent in the English language.

In this story, I chose to simply refer to this character as a 'wealthy young man', instead of constantly referring to him as the 'son of a *boiar*'.

The main point is that this young man comes from a wealthy family, compared to the girl he marries, who may well have been a servant on their estate.

This much higher social status in comparison to his bride gives an indication of the reason why he was able to treat his wife in such a shocking way, simply replacing her with another woman, without anyone from her family intervening on her behalf.

Reading between the lines, this is a story of vindicating a powerless person who has been unjustly treated.

Translating this story made me wonder how often this type of scenario may have occurred for it to become part of a tale told from person to person over a long time.

Finally, the village gathering mentioned towards the end of the story, where the two children tell their story, was a common feature of Romanian rural life.

The inhabitants of the village would often congregate at regular intervals, young and old.

Each person would take turns to entertain the other villagers with their stories.

Indeed, it is likely that this is one way in which the stories you have read in this book, and many other such stories, have been passed down to us through many generations.

I would like to ask you for a small favor.

Reviews are the best way to spread the word about this book.

If you have enjoyed reading this book, it would mean a lot to me if you could leave a review.

Even if you only write a sentence or two, it will help. Thank you!

ABOUT THE AUTHOR

Petre Ispirescu was born in 1830 in Bucharest, where he lived most of his life. He grew up around folk stories, and was greatly inspired by them.

His parents wanted him to become a priest, a career path that required him to start training since childhood.

But at age 14, Ispirescu dropped out of his priest training and took up an apprenticeship at a publishing house.

He was a hard worker and quickly rose through the ranks.

Eventually, he was able to publish his own projects, which is how his collection of fairy tales came about.

He started publishing fairy tales as early as 1862 and continued publishing them over the following two decades.

Sadly, Petre Ispirescu died from a stroke at age 57.

Yet a few of the fairy tales he collected and published are still part of the Romanian literature curriculum to this day.

Alexa Ispas grew up in Romania and moved to Scotland at age 18.

She holds a PhD in psychology from the University of Edinburgh.

Her frequent visits to the Scottish Storytelling Centre inspired her to delve into her Romanian story heritage.

These explorations led her to discover old, forgotten Romanian gems that give us a glimpse into a way of life different from our own.

You can find more of Alexa's translations of old Romanian stories at www.storybothy.com

Jack the Pimple

Can the ugliest boy in the village marry the beautiful princess?

Read this charming story from 19th century Romania, collected by Petre Ispirescu and translated into English by Alexa J Ispas.

Download for free when you sign up to the newsletter at

www.storybothy.com/newsletter